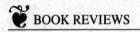 **BOOK REVIEWS**

Here's what people are saying:

*Calhoun presents a dandy adventure here, expertly illustrated by Morrill's drawings.*

from PUBLISHERS WEEKLY

*A suspenseful tale.*

from BOOKLIST

**Weekly Reader Books Presents**

# The Night
# the Monster Came

## MARY CALHOUN

### ILLUSTRATED BY LESLIE MORRILL

William Morrow and Company
New York    1982

## By the Same Author

*Audubon Cat*
*Cross-Country Cat*
*Hot-Air Henry*
and others

This book is a presentation of Weekly Reader Books. Weekly Reader Books offers book clubs for children from preschool through high school. For further information write to: **Weekly Reader Books,** 4343 Equity Drive, Columbus, Ohio 43228.

Published by arrangement with
William Morrow and Company, New York.
Weekly Reader is a trademark of Field Publications.

Library of Congress Cataloging in Publication Data

Calhoun, Mary.
    The night the monster came.
    Summary: After finding giant footprints in the snow, Andy is sure that Bigfoot is stalking his house.
    [1. Bears—Fiction.  2. Sasquatch—Fiction]  I. Morrill, Leslie, ill.
II. Title.                              PZ7.C1278Ni  [Fic]  81-18712
ISBN 0-688-01167-5   ISBN 0-688-01168-3 (lib. bdg.)            AACR2

*To Pinky, the vet,*
*with many thanks.*

# 1

Andy was afraid of monsters.

He was afraid of Frankenstein's monster. He was afraid of giant army ants. But what really scared him was Bigfoot. The man-beast ten feet tall!

Andy was a decent kid who sometimes pulled

younger children in their wagons. He was a decent kid who sometimes lied.

"No, of course I'm not afraid," he said, when his parents left him alone in the house at night.

After all, he was nine years old, too old to be afraid. Not *really* afraid.

All the boys at Cub Scouts said they were scared of Bigfoot.

"Whoo-ee! That big old monster! I wouldn't want to meet him!"

"I'd run like a crazy rabbit!"

"I'd scream! Maybe even faint!"

But they laughed about Bigfoot, too. "I'd take pictures of him and make money." They didn't have to stay alone at night in the last house on the way to the Great North Woods.

Andy's house was the last one on Meadowlark Lane. Beyond were the open fields, and beyond the fields were the woods. Those woods, Andy believed, were the last straggle of wild trees coming down from the Great North Woods.

Where the monsters lived.

In the Great North Woods roamed the Windigo. The Windigo was a shrieking spirit that left

dancing footsteps of fire. And burned-out men. Andy had seen that story on TV.

In the Great North Woods lived Bigfoot. He had wandered into them from the Northwest. He was a huge furry beast, yet he had a face like a man, and he left human footprints nearly two feet long. Andy had seen him on TV, too. The program was a documentary, so it must be true.

One night Andy was alone in the house. His father was working the night shift for the Sheriff's Department, and his mother had to go to real-estate classes that week at the Community Center, a mile away.

"The Trents are home next door," Mom said.

Each house, however, sat on its own half-acre of land, so "next door" wasn't exactly on the other side of the driveway.

"I can be home in three minutes, if you have any trouble," Mom said. "You sure you won't be afraid?"

"Aw, Mom, no!"

Andy grinned and hoped his freckles were staying put. Mom said his freckles stood out when he was scared.

She'd only be going to class three nights, he

reminded himself. It was important. Mom was excited about learning to sell real estate.

After Mom backed the car out, she remembered to work the door-closing device. It rolled the garage door down and locked it automatically. Good old Mom.

Andy checked around. All the doors were locked. All the curtains were drawn against the black night. The telephone worked. He didn't turn on the television, because there might be a scary show. Mom said he watched too much TV, anyway.

Andy settled down to read for his book report. *Stock-Car Racing* was a good safe book to be reading when you're alone in the house.

The house was awfully quiet. Maybe he ought to turn on the television real loud. No, for if there were any strange sounds, he wouldn't hear them.

Andy read on, turned a page.

*Screech.* Andy's heart jumped. A shriek came faintly from outside! The Windigo!

No, he told himself right away. It was an owl. He'd heard that kind of screech before, and it was always an owl.

Just the same, Andy knelt on the couch and peered out between the drapes. It was snowing. A spring snowstorm had set in. Gently snow was beginning to speckle the ground. He couldn't see an owl. Or anything else unusual. The yellow porch light shone softly on the snow.

Andy kept on reading, and his heart quit going so fast. He finished the chapter. Another chapter.

And the garbage can clanged.

It's the neighbor dogs, Andy told himself. The neighbor dogs were after the garbage again.

He went out to the kitchen. Carefully he pinched aside a curtain and peered out at the garbage can. There was a thin layer of snow on the ground.

And in the snow . . . around the garbage can . . . were *giant footprints*.

**Z**

Andy twitched away from the window. His forehead felt cold and damp. His hands were clammy. He stood frozen, listening for sounds. Nothing. Only the whirr of the refrigerator.

He flicked off the kitchen light so he couldn't be seen and looked out the window again. If

Bigfoot was moving around out there, he'd see the figure against the whiteness of the snow. Nothing.

Except those big footprints. They were definitely not dog footprints. They didn't look exactly human either. Long toes with claws. . . . Of course, a monster's footprint would look beastly. And nobody but a monster would run around in the snow barefooted.

He couldn't see through the falling snow whether a trail of prints led *away* from the house.

Breathe. He'd been forgetting to breathe. Andy sucked in breaths softly so nothing could hear him.

Could they *really* be Bigfoot tracks? Maybe Rick Trent next door was playing a late April Fool's joke on him. He'd tell that smart-aleck teen-ager, "April Fool's is done and past, and you're the biggest fool at last!"

Andy looked out the window again at the huge footprints. They were real. There was no way Rick could have faked those footprints.

Where was the monster? He should go through the house and look out other windows.

But what if he *saw* the monster?

Phone Mom! Andy had his hand on the phone. Wait. Bigfoot might get her. No, she'd drive into the garage and use the automatic door-closer. He'd tell her to do that. He'd tell her to bring more people!

But—Andy dithered—the snow was falling fast, already blurring the tracks. What if the footprints were covered by the time people got here? Nobody would believe him.

*Thump, thump*! Feet pounded outside. *Thump, thump*! Andy's heart pounded in his throat. *Clang* went the garbage can.

Snuffling . . . then yipping sounded. This time it was the neighbor dogs. Andy made himself look. Yes, three dogs.

He yelled at them—it felt good to yell—and they raced away, barking. Covering up Bigfoot's tracks. Now the snow around the garbage can was trampled with dog footprints.

What to do? You don't just go back to reading a book after you've seen giant footprints around your house. Andy went to the bathroom.

He didn't hear the garage door open. Dad had oiled and worked on the door to make it move as silently as possible, so it wouldn't wake him when he had to sleep days. The next thing Andy heard was the throb of the car motor in the garage. He tore out of the bathroom.

"Mom, Mom! Close the garage door!" he yelled into the garage from the kitchen door.

Yes, she had. Mom had turned off the ignition; the door was coming down; nobody extra was in the garage.

"Bigfoot is out there! I saw his feet—footprints!"

"Bigfoot!" Mom was laughing. "Andy, you've got to quit watching all that sensational stuff on television. You've got an imagination that won't stop!"

"Really! I saw them! In the s-snow. By the g-garbage c-can."

Andy's teeth were chattering, and finally his mother went to look out the kitchen window. But the snow was all messed up from the dogs' tracks. No Bigfoot prints could be seen.

Andy felt like crying. Bigfoot might still be out there. And even his own mother didn't believe him.

"Okay, Andy," Mom said, "I believe you saw

something, or you wouldn't be this upset. Maybe they were big rabbit tracks."

"Aw, no! I know the difference between rabbit and—and monster tracks."

"Well, there has to be some reasonable explanation," Mom insisted.

"Yeah," said Andy.

# 3

Next day after school Jake and Peter walked from the school bus stop with Andy to his house. They wanted to see the place where the giant footprints had been.

"It snowed some more today," Andy said. "There could be fresh tracks!"

Right then he didn't feel scared at all. It had been exciting to tell everyone at school about the Bigfoot prints. All the kids had wanted to hear his story, and the teacher had to ask them twice to settle down.

The snow was almost knee-deep. Andy led the boys around the side of the house, and they studied the snow for tracks. There were spikey prints where a bird had landed and hopped to a bush. Mouse tracks: a row of tiny dots with a line down the middle where the mouse's tail had trailed. Dog footprints.

"Or maybe a coyote!" said Jake. "Or a bobcat!"

Peter looked worried. "We don't have those around here, do we?"

But there were no monster footprints. The boys searched around the garbage can, but there were no prints, no bits of fur, nothing to show Bigfoot had been there.

"I smell something funny, though," said Jake, sniffing.

"That's just the garbage," Andy said.

Yet the hair on his arms prickled. He smelled something strange too, not exactly a garbage smell.

Peter exclaimed, "And you're going to be alone again tonight? Boy, I wouldn't stay alone where Bigfoot's been stomping around!"

"Well, maybe I—" Andy began. He was about to ask Peter if he'd like to sleep over with him that night.

But Jake was saying, "Naw, Andy's brave. I guess you have to be, when your dad's a sheriff's deputy."

"Yeah," said Andy.

Jake shuffled through the snow, kicking it up. "Probably Bigfoot came out of those woods. Maybe we should go over there and look for tracks. You know, just on the edge of the woods."

The boys looked over the field to the trees. The sky was a dull gray, and the sun was only a faint light spot, low in the grayness. The woods looked deep and lonely.

"No, we'd better not," said Peter. "It'll get dark soon. Looks like it's going to snow again."

Andy was so relieved they weren't going to the woods he said boldly, "Hey, aren't we lucky snow is white? What if snow came down black?"

"Black snow all over!" Jake said.

"Oh, gee! How awful!" Peter shivered.

"Yeah, we'd better get on home."

Jake and Peter left hastily.

Andy went into the house to talk to his father. After school was the only time he got to see him, when Dad worked the night shift. Andy was always asleep when Dad came home after work, and Dad was still asleep in the morning when Andy left to catch the school bus.

Dad buckled the belt on his uniform pants and grinned at Andy. "See any fresh Bigfoot tracks? Your mother told me you've been chasing monsters."

"Aw, come on, Dad! Don't laugh. There really were big tracks last night."

Andy moved things around on the dresser top. Had he *really* seen something?

"Well, let's get Rick Trent to stay with you tonight. Then if Bigfoot comes back, you'll have a witness." Dad pocketed his wallet and keys from the dresser top.

"Oh, geez, don't say that!"

Don't say that Bigfoot is coming back or that

he should have Rick Trent over. Rick was six-
teen and would be sure to tease him about need-
ing a baby-sitter.

"No, I don't want a sitter," Andy said firmly.
"I'll be all right."

Dad shrugged into his jacket. "Tell you what,
son. Bud and I will patrol by here tonight. We'll
check in on you before you go to bed."

"Okay. Good!" Sure as Dad and his partner
came by, there'd be nothing to see. "Hey, I need
a peanut-butter sandwich. See you tonight."

# 4

Andy had never realized how much the house creaked as it settled down for the night. None of the noises sounded in the living room, where he was. The pops and creaks always came from other parts of the house.

It's because of the snow on the roof, he told himself. The weight of the snow makes the timbers creak.

Dad's big chair came up around a person. It was a good place to sit with the stock-car book. Andy set a deadline: he'd finish the book before Dad came by in the patrol truck.

"The track record for Class A cars is—" That noise was just the furnace coming on. "Of all the drivers who—" That whoosh against the window, that was just the wind. "Coming out of the spin, he—"

What was that loud rattle in the kitchen? He'd never heard that sound before. Andy's fingers gripped the book as he listened. *Rattle-rattle.* Something definitely was in the kitchen.

Inside the house!

Run out the front door? No, maybe out there— *Rattle-rustle.*

Andy eased out of the chair and tiptoed toward the kitchen. Ready to run.

The sound came from the garbage sack by the sink. Andy stamped his foot. A mouse ran out of the sack and skittered across the floor.

Dumb mouse! How could a mouse make so much noise?

Andy was sweating. And he was mad at himself. Afraid of a mouse!

He'd better pull himself together and quit being such a scaredy-cat. There was nothing to be afraid of. Probably Bigfoot was just a story, like Dracula. Probably there was some good reason for those tracks he had seen.

Andy thought about calling up Peter to talk awhile. No, he had to finish the book. The report was due the next day.

He had come to the end and was working on the report, when he saw the car lights in the driveway. The patrol truck was here. Snow was falling again, snowflakes flurrying in the headlights. Andy hurried to unlock the door for his father.

"Whoo, those roads are slick!" Dad brushed snow off his coat as he came inside. "Everything all right here?"

"Yeah, sure." Andy's voice was casual. "I'm working on my book report." He'd never tell about the mouse!

"Good. That's my boy." Dad turned to go.

"You coming by again?" Andy kept his voice casual.

"No. We've got a call over at the golf club. Somebody broke in and stole a golf cart. In this snow! Crazy, huh?"

Dad wanted him to laugh, so Andy gave a chuckle.

"Anyway, your mother should be home in an hour. See you tomorrow."

"Okay."

Andy watched the red taillights disappear almost at once in the falling snow. He noted that the house lights were still on at the Trents' down the road. Then he went back to chewing his pencil over the book report.

He got half a page done, but the report was supposed to fill a page. A couple of cookies might help him think. Andy went out to the kitchen. No sign of that idiot mouse. All was silent outside.

Just the same, Andy turned off the kitchen light and looked out the window at the snow around the garbage can. Good. Only a peaceful blanket of snow. No footprints.

He should have gotten his cookies right then.

He shouldn't have kept looking out toward the woods.

There, in the whiteness of the snowstorm, he saw a dark figure. Jumping over the fence into the field was a huge beast.

# 5

"Mom!" Andy yelled into the phone. "I think you better come home right now!"

Even when he told her what he saw, Mom didn't sound convinced. But she agreed to come.

Andy ran upstairs. From the upper windows, he had a better view of the yard around the house. Also, upstairs was farther away from anything that might get in below.

He was panting. Take big breaths, don't faint . . . .

The beast had been no dog. Or person either. Through the falling snow the figure was bulky, furry. Like Bigfoot. Hard to know how tall it was, jumping over the fence between their land and the field.

Afraid to, afraid not to, Andy looked out his bedroom window, over the field, toward the woods. He had the lights off so he could see outside better. The snowfall was letting up. Across the whiteness he could see the dark blur of the woods. No figure, nothing moved anywhere.

In the bathroom, he looked down at the backyard. For a long time he watched a tree, in case something—Something—was hiding behind it. But nothing moved.

He looked out his parents' bedroom window at the front yard and the road. No creature moving on the snowy ground. And no lights of Mom's car coming down the road either.

Andy patrolled from window to window on

the second floor. His clothes were sticking to him, and he didn't make fun of himself for being scared this time. That big dark Thing was no mouse. He *knew* he had seen something.

What a rotten mother and father he had! Leaving a kid alone in a house when there was a monster outside trying to—

He saw headlights on the road. He watched anxiously as Mom drove into the garage. Nothing rushed after the car.

Mom was mad when she came into the kitchen. "All right, where is this monster?"

"Really, I *saw* it—out there by the fence."

"Andy O'Reilly, if you pulled me out of class for nothing—"

"Huh! I suppose you'd like it better if I was dead and gone. That'd prove it to you, I guess!"

To his disgust, he began to cry.

Mom put her arm around his shoulders. "Now, now. Okay, Andy, I believe you. Come on, honey, let's look."

They looked out the kitchen window. The snow was undisturbed around the garbage can. The fence was too far away to tell whether there were tracks where the beast had jumped.

"I suppose the snow is too deep for us to make out footprints around the fence," Andy said, hesitating. They ought to investigate, but—

"Um," said Mom uneasily. "I don't think we should go out there, in case something's still around."

They watched for a long time, but nothing happened. So they went in the living room and talked about it.

"Mom, believe me, it was really *big*."

"But Bigfoot! *That* I can't—"

"At least, it was headed away from here, when it went over the fence."

"Maybe we ought to get a yard light after all."

The O'Reillys had always liked the feeling of living out in the country. They hadn't wanted one of those cold blue lights shining on their house and the field at night.

Andy told his mother about Dad stopping by and the robbery at the golf club.

"Then there's no point in trying to call him," she said.

"I'm sorry you had to miss some of your class."

"Well, it was nearly done."

They watched television until Mom said Andy ought to go to bed. She'd wait up for Dad.

The noise of the television downstairs was comforting, but Andy couldn't go to sleep. As soon as he shut his eyes, he kept seeing the big furry figure going over the fence. That dark shape against the whiteness of the snow. It got taller the more he tried not to think about it.

He was still awake when the pickup truck rumbled into the garage.

Andy flew down the stairs. "Dad! Listen!" He told about the Thing that went over the fence.

"Did he have a golf cart with him?" Dad grinned. "We didn't catch the robber." He took a milk carton out of the refrigerator.

"Oh, geez, Dad!" Andy said bitterly. "You'll pay attention to a dumb robbery, and you won't even believe something fantastic is happening in your own yard!"

"We didn't want to go clear out to the fence to look for tracks," Mom put in. "Now it's too late." More snow had fallen.

"All right, I'm sorry you were scared," Dad apologized. "I guess you're both scared."

He said in the morning he would call the office

and ask "the boys" to check out the woods across the field. There was access to the woods from one of the county roads.

"And I'm going to ask Rick Trent to stay with you tomorrow night," Mom told Andy.

Andy didn't argue.

# 6

The storm was over. Sun sparkled on snow that lay soft and smooth, like miles of vanilla ice cream. The gully behind Jake's house was perfect for sledding.

"I'll get my sled. Be right back!"

Andy raced down Meadowlark Lane toward

his house. A plow had been through, and snow was banked up along the sides of the road. Romping in the snow were two of the neighborhood dogs, rooting their noses in the white stuff and snorting, kicking up snow with their hind legs—glorious, glorious! Andy tousled the black lab's ears, then stopped, because there was a cut on the dog's head.

The Trents' redbone hound wasn't playing with the dogs. Andy saw Rover lying on the Trents' porch, tied up. And no wonder. Three deep scratches ran down the dog's shoulder and flank. Rover looked miserable.

Andy stood still in the snowy road. What had gashed up the dogs? The night they had chased something from the garbage can—Something——

Ahh! Andy shook his head and ran on. The day was too cheery for imagining scary things When dogs ran in a pack, they could get into any kind of trouble.

There was a gay mob scene of birds at Andy's house. Good old Mom had remembered to take care of the birds after the snowstorm. Chickadees chattered at the birdfeeder filled with sunflower seeds, and jays pecked at a net bag of suet hung from the porch roof.

"Hey, I'm home! But I'm going sledding over at Jake's, okay?"

Mom was studying a fat book on real estate law at the desk in the living room. She sighed wearily, pushing back her hair.

"Andy, Mrs. Trent said Rick has a basketball game tonight, an all-state conference game. And the Trents are going to it. I was waiting until after school to try to get some other teen-ager to stay with you."

"Huh. Well, why don't you just skip it? I think everything's going to be okay now." Andy grinned and punched her shoulder to prove he was all right.

"What? Even though you were so scared last night?"

"Yeah, well—I've been thinking. I've been imagining too many things about monsters. Probably what I saw was just a tree shadow made by car lights over on the highway."

At school, the kids had asked if he'd seen any more of the big tracks, and suddenly he had realized he didn't want to talk about Bigfoot. If the monster was real, it was too scary to dis-cuss. If he'd just imagined things, then he didn't want to admit he'd been a coward.

It was time he quit building things up and used common sense, Andy told himself. Look at all the good things: the sun was shining, and it was Friday. He had the whole weekend to play out in the snow. Tonight was Mom's last class, and Dad would be on day shift next week.

"You could come to the class with me," Mom was saying. "Now I'm really worried about leav-ing you alone."

"Or you could ask Jake to spend the night here," Dad said, coming out of the kitchen with his lunch box.

"Aw, no!" Andy said to both of them. He didn't want to go to that boring class, and if Jake came over, he'd be sure to tell ghost stories. Jake was always proving how brave he was.

And besides—

"Look, see," Andy tried to explain to them, "after tonight it won't matter, because you guys will be around. I've only got one more chance to be brave."

Andy loved the way his dad's whole face

curled upward when he smiled. "Son, you're all right."

Then Dad added, "The boys didn't find anything in the woods today. Oh, they saw plenty of animal tracks, plus some blood where a fox must have gotten a rabbit. Jerry said there was a plowed-up trail where some kind of commotion had gone on. But they waited and walked around quite awhile, and they didn't see anything strange moving about."

"That's good," Andy said slowly.

As Dad had talked, Andy had been picturing the deputies chasing down a man-beast in the snowy woods. Bigfoot trapped. And it was all wrong.

Somehow he wanted to believe in Bigfoot. Yet not *really* believe he'd come right up to a person's garbage can. He shouldn't be caught. Bigfoot ought to keep on being a mystery monster, roaming free in the woods.

Still, what if a real monster had been hiding from the deputies, very still somewhere, watching—

Now, cut that out! Andy went out in the sunshine with his sled.

# 7

Andy's body felt pleasantly tired from the work-out in the snow. He was about to turn off the TV and go to bed early, when he heard the thumping.

Something was thumping against the house.

Oh, no! He was trying not to imagine things.

He was *trying* to be sensible and brave, and things wouldn't cooperate!

*Thump-bump*.

It's a tree branch. The wind is blowing a tree branch against the house. (His heart was going *thump-bump*, too.) Or it's the neighbor dogs. The dogs are after the garbage again.

Except that Mom had brought the garbage can inside, in case it was attracting something. And the bumping and brushing sounds weren't out in back. The sounds were in front, right on the other side of the living-room wall.

Run upstairs and hide in a closet!

Like a scaredy-cat.

All right, then, I'll just look!

Andy made his legs walk to the front door. He made his eyes look out the narrow window slit up and down in the door.

And he saw fur.

His head felt light. Sparks flashed in his eyes. He was going to faint.

Instead, the fur started to slide down. Next the *face* would look in the window at him.

Andy didn't wait. He flew to the telephone and dialed the Sheriff's Department.

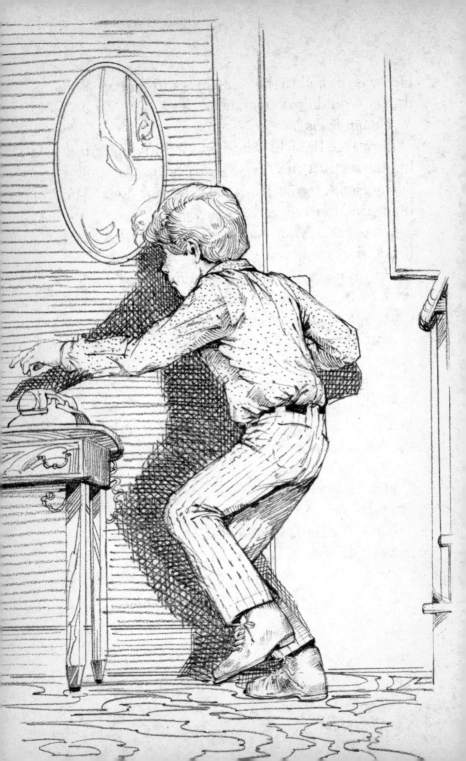

"This is Andy O'Reilly!" he shrilled into the phone. "Tell my dad to come home right away! There's a—a prowler at our house!"

He didn't dare say "a monster, Bigfoot." The dispatcher wouldn't believe him, might not tell Dad.

No fur showed now at the window in the door. But out there on the porch the Thing was breathing. Panting. Fast, heavy panting sounds. Andy whirled to race up the stairs and hide.

Then he stopped. I have to know what it is, he thought to himself.

Oh, why did he have to feel that way! Yet his feet carried him tiptoeing toward the front door.

He heard the husky panting. He saw a hump of fur lying on the porch. And blood on the snow that had blown up on the porch. The hump of fur moved. Andy jumped back, but he saw what it was.

It wasn't Bigfoot. It was a bear.

Between the bear's paws was the net bag of suet Mom had hung out for the birds. The bear gulped the last of the fat and panted.

"Good—golly!" Andy breathed. Those

woods across the field really were wild woods. A big black bear lived in those woods!

The bear had waked up hungry in the spring . . . the garbage can . . . Andy's mind raced. The long claw toes of the footprints . . . the dogs . . . . They had caught up with the bear! That's why the dogs were clawed up. That's why the bear's leg was bleeding.

Under the soft yellow porch light, the bear sat up and licked the hind leg where new blood trickled through the hair. The leg was badly torn, and the fur around the wounds was licked slimy.

Andy chewed at a fingernail. Maybe the bear would die, if the bleeding wasn't stopped. Pressure, he remembered from Cub Scout training. Pressure on the wounds with a tight bandage could stop the bleeding. If he got a dish towel—

No way! When Dad was grouchy, Mom said he was "as cross as a wounded bear." That bear would mangle him, if he tried to get near the bleeding leg. The bear would have to be tranquilized. Then a veterinarian could—

The bear looked at the front door. Would it jump, raging, at the door, pound it down?

Andy's body didn't move, but his heart inside was leaping.

The bear moaned and slumped down over its hurt leg. The creature could be weak from loss of blood. Probably walking across the field and jumping over the barbed-wire fence had made the wounds bleed more. And standing up to claw down the bag of suet.

Very quietly Andy stepped back from the door. What should he do? Do you just leave a bear bleeding to death on your front porch?

Of course, Dad would get there soon, and then he—

Dad! Andy's hand flew to his mouth. He pictured Dad jumping out of the patrol truck and the wounded bear charging at Dad.

Somehow he had to stop the bear, trap the bear, before Dad drove up.

**8**

How to trap the bear? Andy thought fast. A blanket. When the patrol truck came, he could throw a blanket over the bear.

Andy ran up the stairs to get a blanket. Halfway up he thought, No, that's too tricky. When he opened the door to throw the blanket, the bear might get him first. Andy ran down the stairs. If only he had someplace to pen up the bear . . . .

The garage! Somehow he had to coax the bear into the garage. Coax? "Here, bear-y-bear!" Andy almost giggled, he felt so keyed up. Let's see, bears like bacon . . . .

Andy grabbed a package of bacon from the refrigerator. He flicked the switch that opened the garage door. The tracks were as well oiled as ever, and he heard just the quietest sound of the door rolling up. Had the bear been startled by the sound? Bacon in hand, Andy tiptoed to the front door and peered out the window slit.

The black bear still lay on the porch, panting with pain and bleeding.

Andy unlocked the kitchen door to the garage, and he left the door open, so he could make a fast re-entry. Then, silently, carefully, he dropped a trail of bacon strips on the garage floor to the front.

Now came the hard part, when the bear could see him. Yet he had to call the bear's attention to the bacon. Andy stepped just outside the garage and tossed a strip of bacon onto the porch.

The bear saw the bacon! The head lifted, round furry ears stood up, close-together eyes looked, muzzle of a nose sniffed . . . . Andy plopped another strip of bacon on the walkway to the garage and then ran like a crazy thing. On tiptoe.

Back in the kitchen, he remembered not to slam the door. Don't startle the bear. If only the bear was hungry enough to follow the bacon right into a human being's building! At least, there was no light in the garage to warn him it was a strange place.

Andy leaned against the kitchen door, listening. No sound. Then he heard a kind of whuffling snort. Turning off the kitchen lights, he opened the door a crack and peeked out.

Through the darkness, he saw the shape of the bear just outside the garage. On its feet the bear looked huge! He swung his head from side to side, sniffing. A strip of bacon lay ahead on the garage pavement. The bear moved forward. Hobbled.

Andy's mouth pinched together when he saw how painfully the poor old bear moved, dragging one mangled leg behind him. Maybe a muscle or tendon was torn.

The bear ate the bacon. Actually, the bear seemed to inhale the bacon. Andy almost laughed as he watched the bear slurp the strip into his mouth. Those were fierce-looking teeth, though.

Follow the trail, follow the trail, Andy willed.

The furry head turned, looking behind. Leaving? No, just checking. The bear hobbled to the next bacon strip.

Wait, wait! Andy said to himself. The bear had to come far inside the garage, nearly to the kitchen door before he dared flick the switch. Surely the bear would hear or see the door coming down and would try to get out. The bad leg made him move slowly, but the door didn't come down like a snap either.

Finger on the switch, Andy waited while the bear ate its way closer . . . and closer . . . . He breathed as softly as he could, to keep the bear from hearing him. One hand held the door, ready to slam it shut, if he had to. Oh, what if the bear smelled him?

The bear's nose followed the bacon . . . nearly up to the workbench . . . *slurp*, went a bacon strip . . . .

Now! Andy worked the switch, and the garage door began to slide down.

The bear half turned, saw the door moving. He lumbered toward the entrance to get away. Too late! The door shut down, almost on the bear's nose. Got him! Andy had trapped a bear!

He felt a moment's pity at the way the bear's body whirled around, the claws scraping at the door, the panic the bear must be feeling.

That's all right, fella. Now you'll get help, he thought.

Andy locked the kitchen door. Should he drag the kitchen table up against it, in case the bear was strong enough to pound in the door? The trapped creature bellowed. Andy's knees almost gave way.

Then he heard a car motor. Oh, for goodness sakes, not Mom! She couldn't open the garage again with her automatic switch!

Andy ran out the front door, yelling, "Hey, hey!"

But it was the sheriff's department truck. Dad jumped out.

"Andy, are you all right?"

"Hey, Dad! Have you got a tranquilizer gun? You won't believe what I've got in the garage!"

*g*

The rest was tricky too.

   Dad's partner, Bud, radioed for a veterinarian with a tranquilizer gun. Then they waited out in the snowy night with the headlights shining on the garage door. They could hear the bear growling and clawing and thumping at the door. Andy felt sorry for the bear, and Dad said he hated to think what his garage was going to look like.

"I intend to discuss this with you, young man!" Dad had begun. "You shouldn't have fooled with that bear!"

But Andy had explained how the bear would have charged on Dad. And all Dad could do was shake his head and exclaim, "Andy, you are —I don't know whether to spank you or thank you!"

When the veterinarian drove up in his van, there was a glare of headlights on the garage door. The vet got out, carrying a capture gun that looked like a .410 shotgun. It was loaded with a projectile filled with tranquilizer. Dad and Bud stood ready with their guns, in case the bear tried to attack before the tranquilizer could take effect.

"Don't kill him!" Andy begged.

Dad told him, "Go inside and work the garage door switch."

Inside, Andy listened at the kitchen door. The bear was scraping and grunting. Andy turned the switch and eased the door open a crack for one last look at his bear.

Great furry creature, the most fantastic sight he had ever seen. Live, not on TV.

As the garage door moved upward, the bear stood frozen in the sudden glare of headlights. The vet's tranquilizer gun zinged, and the bear flinched. He bit at his shoulder where the dart had gone into a muscle. Then the bear roared and ran.

"He's getting away!" Andy wailed. He started into the garage.

"Stay there!" his father yelled at him.

So Andy rushed to the kitchen window in time to see the bear lumber across the yard toward the field. At the fence, the poor beast made two tries before he got over it. The men turned the cars so their headlights shone over the field.

Halfway to the woods, the bear dropped.

It was a job for the three men to pull the bear back across the field in the snow. Dad and Bud grabbed the shoulders, and the vet tried to ease along the rear without harming the wounded leg. All Andy could do to help was hold a flashlight in each hand. The bear was out cold.

"He must weigh four hundred pounds!" the vet exclaimed.

"But what's he *doing* here? Close to houses," Bud asked, puffing.

"Must have been confused by the storm—and hungry," answered the vet, breathing hard. "Bears will go back to known food sources. I'll get his leg fixed up. Then the fish-and-game people can drop him off in deeper woods, where he won't be tempted to raid garbage cans."

Huffing, Dad stopped to rest with the others. "What I want to know is, how'd you have the nerve to trap him, Andy? Weren't you scared?"

"Yeah! At first, when I saw that fur on the porch, I almost fainted!" Andy chattered. "And when I saw that big old bear and thought about him getting you—"

Andy looked down at the mound of fur in the snow. He shone a flashlight on the bear's snout, the closed eyes. His bear.

"But after that," he said slowly, "I guess I was thinking too fast to have time to be scared."

Mom drove up just as they were lifting the bear into the vet's van. "What on earth!"

Andy called out to her, "See? I told you a big beast was hanging around our house! And I caught him!"

"Bigfoot?" Her face was white in the head-lights.

"Aw, no, Mom. A bear!"

Andy's knees felt watery with relief as he realized something. He would have been ashamed to have caught Bigfoot, that wild free mystery monster.

## About the Author

Born in Keokuk, Iowa, Mary Calhoun received a B.A. degree in journalism at the State University of Iowa, and for some years after graduation worked as a reporter on newspapers in the Midwest and far West. She lives with her husband, the Reverend Leon Wilkins, in Steamboat Springs, Colorado, a small town in the Rockies. A well-known children's author, Ms. Calhoun 'has written picture books, stories for eight- to twelve-year-olds, and teen-age novels.

## About the Illustrator

A native of Nashua, New Hampshire, Leslie Morrill holds a degree of B.S. Ed. from Tufts University in Medford, Massachusetts, an M.F.A. degree from Cranbrook Academy of Art in Bloomfield Hills, Michigan, and attended an undergraduate program at the Boston Museum of Fine Arts. Since then Mr. Morrill has taught, served as an art consultant, and worked as a free-lance illustrator. Presently he and his wife and daughter live in Wellesley, Massachusetts.